PENG

THE GREE
COFFE

Stephen King, one of the world's bestselling writers, was born in Portland, Maine, in 1947, and was educated at the University of Maine at Orono. He shot to fame with the publication of his first novel, *Carrie*, and his subsequent titles include *The Shining* and *Misery*, which have all been made into highly successful films. He lives with his wife, the novelist Tabitha King, and their three children in Bangor, Maine.

Watch out for Stephen King's *Rose Madder*, out soon in paperback from New English Library, and his new novel *Desperation*, coming shortly in hardback from Hodder & Stoughton.

Coffey's Hands is the third in a novel of six parts. The first two volumes, *The Two Dead Girls* and *The Mouse on the Mile*, are also published in Penguin.

STEPHEN KING

The Green Mile

PART THREE

Coffey's Hands

PENGUIN BOOKS

PENGUIN BOOKS

Published by the Penguin Group
Penguin Books Ltd, 27 Wrights Lane, London W8 5TZ, England
Penguin Books USA Inc., 375 Hudson Street, New York, New York 10014, USA
Penguin Books Australia Ltd, Ringwood, Victoria, Australia
Penguin Books Canada Ltd, 10 Alcorn Avenue, Toronto, Ontario, Canada M4V 3B2
Penguin Books (NZ) Ltd, 182–190 Wairau Road, Auckland 10, New Zealand

Penguin Books Ltd, Registered Offices: Harmondsworth, Middlesex, England

Published simultaneously in the USA in Signet and
in Great Britain in Penguin Books 1996
3 5 7 9 10 8 6 4 2

Printed in England by Clays Ltd, St Ives plc

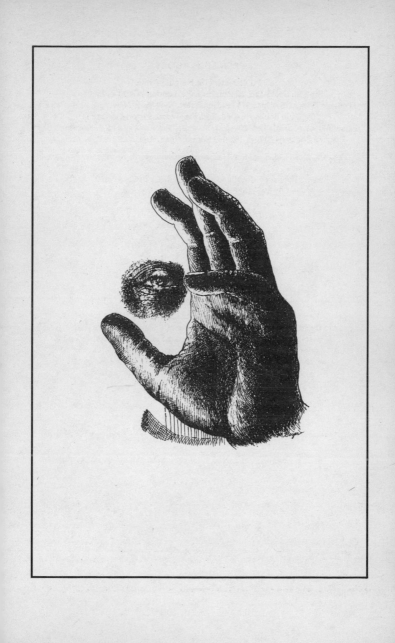

1

Looking back through what I've written, I see that I called Georgia Pines, where I now live, a nursing home. The folks who run the place wouldn't be very happy with that! According to the brochures they keep in the lobby and send out to prospective clients, it's a "state-of-the-art retirement complex for the elderly." It even has a Resource Center—the brochure says so. The folks who have to live here (the brochure doesn't call us "inmates," but sometimes I do) just call it the TV room.

Folks think I'm stand-offy because I don't go down to the TV room much in the day, but it's the programs I can't stand, not the folks. Oprah, Ricki Lake, Carnie Wilson, Rolanda—the world is falling down around our ears, and all these people care for is talking about fucking to women in short skirts and men with their shirts hanging open. Well, hell—judge not, lest ye be judged, the Bible says, so I'll get down off my soapbox. It's just that if I wanted to spend time with trailer trash, I'd move two miles down to the Happy Wheels Motor Court, where the police cars always seem to be headed on Friday and Saturday nights with their sirens screaming and their blue lights flashing. My special friend, Elaine Connelly, feels the same way. Elaine is eighty, tall and slim, still erect and clear-eyed, very intelligent and refined. She walks very slowly because there's something wrong with her hips, and I know that the arthritis in her hands gives her terrible misery, but she has a beautiful long neck—a swan neck, almost—and long, pretty hair that falls to her shoulders when she lets it down.

Best of all, she doesn't think I'm peculiar, or stand-offy. We spend a lot of time together, Elaine and I. If I hadn't reached such a grotesque age, I suppose I might speak of her as my ladyfriend. Still, having a special friend—just that—is not so bad, and in some ways, it's even better. A lot of the problems and heartaches that go with being boyfriend and girlfriend have simply burned out of us. And although I know that no one under the age of, say, fifty would believe this, sometimes the embers are better than the campfire. It's strange, but it's true.

So I don't watch TV during the day. Sometimes I walk; sometimes I read; mostly what I've been doing for the last month or so is writing this memoir among the plants in the solarium. I think there's more oxygen in that room, and it helps the old memory. It beats the hell out of Geraldo Rivera, I can tell you that.

But when I can't sleep, I sometimes creep downstairs and put on the television. There's no Home Box

Office or anything at Georgia Pines—I guess that's a resource just a wee bit too expensive for our Resource Center—but we have the basic cable services, and that means we have the American Movie Channel. That's the one (just in case you don't have the basic cable services yourself) where most of the films are in black and white and none of the women take their clothes off. For an old fart like me, that's sort of soothing. There have been a good many nights when I've slipped right off to sleep on the ugly green sofa in front of the TV while Francis the Talking Mule once more pulls Donald O'Connor's skillet out of the fire, or John Wayne cleans up Dodge, or Jimmy Cagney calls someone a dirty rat and then pulls a gun. Some of them are movies I saw with my wife, Janice (not just my ladyfriend but my *best* friend), and they calm me. The clothes they wear, the way they walk and talk, even the music on the soundtrack—all those things calm me. They remind me, I suppose, of when I was a man still walking on the skin of the world, instead of a moth-eaten relic mouldering away in an old folks' home where many of the residents wear diapers and rubber pants.

There was nothing soothing about what I saw this morning, though. Nothing at all.

Elaine sometimes joins me for AMC's so-called Early Bird Matinee, which starts at 4:00 a.m.—she doesn't say much about it, but I know her arthritis hurts her something terrible, and that the drugs they give her don't help much anymore.

When she came in this morning, gliding like a

ghost in her white terrycloth robe, she found me sitting on the lumpy sofa, bent over the scrawny sticks that used to be legs, and clutching my knees to try and still the shakes that were running through me like a high wind. I felt cold all over, except for my groin, which seemed to burn with the ghost of the urinary infection which had so troubled my life in the fall of 1932—the fall of John Coffey, Percy Wetmore, and Mr. Jingles, the trained mouse.

The fall of William Wharton, it had been, too.

"Paul!" Elaine cried, and hurried over to me— hurried as fast as the rusty nails and ground glass in her hips would allow, anyway. "Paul, what's wrong?"

"I'll be all right," I said, but the words didn't sound very convincing—they came out all uneven, through teeth that wanted to chatter. "Just give me a minute or two, I'll be right as rain."

She sat next to me and put her arm around my shoulders. "I'm sure," she said. "But what happened? For heaven's sake, Paul, you look like you saw a ghost."

I did, I thought, and didn't realize until her eyes widened that I'd said it out loud.

"Not really," I said, and patted her hand (gently—so gently!). "But for a minute, Elaine— God!"

"Was it from the time when you were a guard at the prison?" she asked. "The time that you've been writing about in the solarium?"

I nodded. "I worked on our version of Death Row—"

"I know—"

"Only we called it the Green Mile. Because of the linoleum on the floor. In the fall of '32, we got this fellow—we got this *wildman*—named William Wharton. Liked to think of himself as Billy the Kid, even had it tattooed on his arm. Just a kid, but dangerous. I can still remember what Curtis Anderson— he was the assistant warden back in those days— wrote about him. 'Crazy-wild and proud of it. Wharton is nineteen years old, and *he just doesn't care.*' He'd underlined that part."

The hand which had gone around my shoulders was now rubbing my back. I was beginning to calm. In that moment I loved Elaine Connelly, and could have kissed her all over her face as I told her so. Maybe I should have. It's terrible to be alone and frightened at any age, but I think it's worst when you're old. But I had this other thing on my mind, this load of old and still unfinished business.

"Anyway," I said, "you're right—I've been scribbling about how Wharton came on the block and almost killed Dean Stanton—one of the guys I worked with back then—when he did."

"How could he do that?" Elaine asked.

"Meanness and carelessness," I said grimly. "Wharton supplied the meanness, and the guards who brought him in supplied the carelessness. The real mistake was Wharton's wrist-chain—it was a little too long. When Dean unlocked the door to E

Block, Wharton was behind him. There were guards on either side of him, but Anderson was right—Wild Billy just didn't care about such things. He dropped that wrist-chain down over Dean's head and started choking him with it."

Elaine shuddered.

"Anyway, I got thinking about all that and couldn't sleep, so I came down here. I turned on AMC, thinking you might come down and we'd have us a little date—"

She laughed and kissed my forehead just above the eyebrow. It used to make me prickle all over when Janice did that, and it still made me prickle all over when Elaine did it early this morning. I guess some things don't ever change.

"—and what came on was this old black-and-white gangster movie from the forties. *Kiss of Death*, it's called."

I could feel myself wanting to start shaking again and tried to suppress it.

"Richard Widmark's in it," I said. "It was his first big part, I think. I never went to see it with Jan—we gave the cops and robbers a miss, usually—but I remember reading somewhere that Widmark gave one hell of a performance as the punk. He sure did. He's pale . . . doesn't seem to walk so much as go *gliding* around . . . he's always calling people 'squirt' . . . talking about squealers . . . how much he hates the squealers . . ."

I was starting to shiver again in spite of my best efforts. I just couldn't help it.

"Blond hair," I whispered. "Lank blond hair. I watched until the part where he pushed this old woman in a wheelchair down a flight of stairs, then I turned it off."

"He reminded you of Wharton?"

"He *was* Wharton," I said. "To the life."

"Paul—" she began, and stopped. She looked at the blank screen of the TV (the cable box on top of it was still on, the red numerals still showing 10, the number of the AMC channel), then back at me.

"What?" I asked. "What, Elaine?" Thinking, *She's going to tell me I ought to quit writing about it. That I ought to tear up the pages I've written so far and just quit on it.*

What she said was "Don't let this stop you."

I gawped at her.

"Close your mouth, Paul—you'll catch a fly."

"Sorry. It's just that . . . well . . ."

"You thought I was going to tell you just the opposite, didn't you?"

"Yes."

She took my hands in hers (gently, so gently—her long and beautiful fingers, her bunched and ugly knuckles) and leaned forward, fixing my blue eyes with her hazel ones, the left slightly dimmed by the mist of a coalescing cataract. "I may be too old and brittle to live," she said, "but I'm not too old to think. What's a few sleepless nights at our age? What's seeing a ghost on the TV, for that matter? Are you going to tell me it's the only one you've ever seen?"

I thought about Warden Moores, and Harry

Terwilliger, and Brutus Howell; I thought about my mother, and about Jan, my wife, who died in Alabama. I knew about ghosts, all right.

"No," I said. "It wasn't the first ghost I've ever seen. But Elaine—it *was* a shock. Because it was *him*."

She kissed me again, then stood up, wincing as she did so and pressing the heels of her hands to the tops of her hips, as if she were afraid they might actually explode out through her skin if she wasn't very careful.

"I think I've changed my mind about the television," she said. "I've got an extra pill that I've been keeping for a rainy day . . . or night. I think I'll take it and go back to bed. Maybe you should do the same."

"Yes," I said. "I suppose I should." For one wild moment I thought of suggesting that we go back to bed together, and then I saw the dull pain in her eyes and thought better of it. Because she might have said yes, and she would only have said that for me. Not so good.

We left the TV room (I won't dignify it with that other name, not even to be ironic) side by side, me matching my steps to hers, which were slow and painfully careful. The building was quiet except for someone moaning in the grip of a bad dream behind some closed door.

"Will you be able to sleep, do you think?" she asked.

"Yes, I think so," I said, but of course I wasn't able to; I lay in my bed until sunup, thinking about *Kiss of Death.* I'd see Richard Widmark, giggling madly, tying the old lady into her wheelchair and then pushing her down the stairs—"This is what we do to squealers," he told her—and then his face would merge into the face of William Wharton as he'd looked on the day when he came to E Block and the Green Mile—Wharton giggling like Widmark, Wharton screaming, *Ain't this a party, now? Is it, or what?* I didn't bother with breakfast, not after that; I just came down here to the solarium and began to write.

Ghosts? Sure.

I know all about ghosts.

2

"Whooooee, boys!" Wharton laughed. "*Ain't this a party, now? Is it, or what?*"

Still screaming and laughing, Wharton went back to choking Dean with his chain. Why not? Wharton knew what Dean and Harry and my friend Brutus Howell knew—they could only fry a man once.

"Hit him!" Harry Terwilliger screamed. He had grappled with Wharton, tried to stop things before they got fairly started, but Wharton had thrown him off and now Harry was trying to find his feet. "Percy, hit him!"

But Percy only stood there, hickory baton in hand, eyes as wide as soup-plates. He loved that damned baton of his, and you would have said this was the chance to use it he'd been pining for ever since he came to Cold Mountain Penitentiary . . . but now that it had come, he was too scared to use the opportunity. This wasn't some terrified little Frenchman like Delacroix or a black giant who hardly seemed to know he was in his own body, like John Coffey; this was a whirling devil.

I came out of Wharton's cell, dropping my clip-board and pulling my .38. For the second time that day I had forgotten the infection that was heating up my middle. I didn't doubt the story the others told of Wharton's blank face and dull eyes when they recounted it later, but that wasn't the Wharton I saw. What I saw was the face of an animal—not an intelligent animal, but one filled with cunning ... and meanness ... and joy. Yes. He was doing what he had been made to do. The place and the circumstances didn't matter. The other thing I saw was Dean Stanton's red, swelling face. He was dying in front of my eyes. Wharton saw the gun in my hand and turned Dean toward it, so that I'd almost certainly have to hit one to hit the other. From over Dean's shoulder, one blazing blue eye dared me to shoot. Wharton's other eye was hidden by Dean's hair. Behind them I saw Percy standing irresolute, with his baton half-raised. And then, filling the open doorway to the prison yard, a miracle in the flesh: Brutus Howell. They had finished moving the last of the infirmary equipment, and he had come over to see who wanted coffee.

He acted without a moment's hesitation—shoved Percy aside and into the wall with tooth-rattling force, pulled his own baton out of its loop, and brought it crashing down on the back of Wharton's head with all the force in his massive right arm. There was a dull *whock*! sound—an almost hollow sound, as if there were no brain at all under Wharton's skull—and the chain finally loosened around

Dean's neck. Wharton went down like a sack of meal and Dean crawled away, hacking harshly and holding one hand to his throat, his eyes bulging.

I knelt by him and he shook his head violently. "Okay," he rasped. "Take care . . . him!" He motioned at Wharton. "Lock! Cell!"

I didn't think he'd need a cell, as hard as Brutal had hit him; I thought he'd need a coffin. No such luck, though. Wharton was conked out, but a long way from dead. He lay sprawled on his side, one arm thrown out so that the tips of his fingers touched the linoleum of the Green Mile, his eyes shut, his breathing slow but regular. There was even a peaceful little smile on his face, as if he'd gone to sleep listening to his favorite lullaby. A tiny red rill of blood was seeping out of his hair and staining the collar of his new prison shirt. That was all.

"Percy," I said. "Help me!"

Percy didn't move, only stood against the wall, staring with wide, stunned eyes. I don't think he knew exactly where he was.

"Percy, goddammit, grab hold of him!"

He got moving, then, and Harry helped him. Together the three of us hauled the unconscious Mr. Wharton into his cell while Brutal helped Dean to his feet and held him as gently as any mother while Dean bent over and hacked air back into his lungs.

Our new problem child didn't wake up for almost three hours, but when he did, he showed absolutely no ill effects from Brutal's savage hit. He came to the way he moved—fast. At one moment he was lying on his bunk, dead to the world. At the next he was standing at the bars—he was silent as a cat—and staring out at me as I sat at the duty desk, writing a report on the incident. When I finally sensed someone looking at me and glanced up, there he was, his grin displaying a set of blackening, dying teeth with several gaps among them already. It gave me a jump to see him there like that. I tried not to show it, but I think he knew. "Hey, flunky," he said. "Next time it'll be you. And I won't miss."

"Hello, Wharton," I said, as evenly as I could. "Under the circumstances, I guess I can skip the speech and the Welcome Wagon, don't you think?"

His grin faltered just a little. It wasn't the sort of response he had expected, and probably wasn't the one I would have given under other circumstances. But something had happened while Wharton was unconscious. It is, I suppose, one of the major things I have trudged through all these pages to tell you about. Now let's just see if you believe it.

3

Except for shouting once at Delacroix, Percy kept his mouth shut once the excitement was over. This was probably the result of shock rather than any effort at tact—Percy Wetmore knew as much about tact as I do about the native tribes of darkest Africa, in my opinion—but it was a damned good thing, just the same. If he'd started in whining about how Brutal had pushed him into the wall or wondering why no one had told him that nasty men like Wild Billy Wharton sometimes turned up on E Block, I think we would have killed him. Then we could have toured the Green Mile in a whole new way. That's sort of a funny idea, when you consider it. I missed my chance to make like James Cagney in *White Heat*.

Anyway, when we were sure that Dean was going to keep breathing and that he wasn't going to pass out on the spot, Harry and Brutal escorted him over to the infirmary. Delacroix, who had been absolutely silent during the scuffle (he had been in prison lots of times, that one, and knew when it was prudent to keep his yap shut and when it was relatively safe to open it again), began bawling loudly down the corridor as Harry and Brutal helped Dean out. Delacroix wanted to know what had happened. You would have thought his constitutional rights had been violated.

"Shut up, you little queer!" Percy yelled back, so furious that the veins stood out on the sides of his neck. I put a hand on his arm and felt it quivering beneath his shirt. Some of this was residual fright, of course (every now and then I had to remind myself that part of Percy's problem was that he was only twenty-one, not much older than Wharton), but I think most of it was rage. He hated Delacroix. I don't know just why, but he did.

"Go see if Warden Moores is still here," I told Percy. "If he is, give him a complete verbal report on what happened. Tell him he'll have my written report on his desk tomorrow, if I can manage it."

Percy swelled visibly at this responsibility; for a horrible moment or two, I actually thought he might salute. "Yes, sir. I will."

"Begin by telling him that the situation in E Block is normal. It's not a story, and the warden won't appreciate you dragging it out to heighten the suspense."

"I won't."

"Okay. Off you go."

He started for the door, then turned back. The one thing you could count on with him was contrariness. I desperately wanted him gone, my groin was on fire, and now he didn't seem to want to go.

"Are you all right, Paul?" he asked. "Running a fever, maybe? Got a touch of the grippe? Cause there's sweat all over your face."

"I might have a touch of something, but mostly I'm fine," I said. "Go on, Percy, tell the warden."

He nodded and left—thank Christ for small favors. As soon as the door was closed, I lunged into my office. Leaving the duty desk unmanned was against regulations, but I was beyond caring about that. It was bad—like it had been that morning.

I managed to get into the little toilet cubicle behind the desk and to get my business out of my pants before the urine started to gush, but it was a near thing. I had to put a hand over my mouth to stifle a scream as I began to flow, and grabbed blindly for the lip of the washstand with the other. It wasn't like my house, where I could fall to my knees and piss a puddle beside the woodpile; if I went to my knees here, the urine would go all over the floor.

I managed to keep my feet and not to scream, but it was a close thing on both counts. It felt like my urine had been filled with tiny slivers of broken glass. The smell coming up from the toilet bowl was swampy and unpleasant, and I could see white stuff—pus, I guess—floating on the surface of the water.

I took the towel off the rack and wiped my face with it. I was sweating, all right; it was pouring off me. I looked into the metal mirror and saw the flushed face of a man running a high fever looking back at me. Hundred and three? Hundred and four?

Better not to know, maybe. I put the towel back on its bar, flushed the toilet, and walked slowly back across my office to the cellblock door. I was afraid Bill Dodge or someone else might have come in and seen three prisoners with no attendants, but the place was empty. Wharton still lay unconscious on his bunk, Delacroix had fallen silent, and John Coffey had never made a single noise at all, I suddenly realized. Not a peep. Which was worrisome.

I went down the Mile and glanced into Coffey's cell, half-expecting to discover he'd committed suicide in one of the two common Death Row ways—either hanging himself with his pants, or gnawing into his wrists. No such thing, it turned out. Coffey merely sat on the end of his bunk with his hands in his lap, the largest man I'd ever seen in my life, looking at me with his strange, wet eyes.

"Cap'n?" he said.

"What's up, big boy?"

"I need to see you."

"Ain't you looking right at me, John Coffey?"

He said nothing to this, only went on studying me with his strange, leaky gaze. I sighed.

"In a second, big boy."

I looked over at Delacroix, who was standing at the bars of his cell. Mr. Jingles, his pet mouse (Delacroix would tell you he'd trained Mr. Jingles to do tricks, but us folks who worked on the Green Mile were pretty much unanimous in the opinion that Mr. Jingles had trained himself), was jumping restlessly back and forth from one of Del's outstretched hands to the other, like an acrobat doing leaps from platforms high above the center ring. His eyes were huge, his ears laid back against his sleek brown skull. I hadn't any doubt that the mouse was reacting to Delacroix's nerves. As I watched, he ran down Delacroix's pantsleg and across the cell to where the brightly colored spool lay against one wall. He pushed the spool back to Delacroix's foot and then looked up at him eagerly, but the little Cajun took no notice of his friend, at least for the time being.

"What happen, boss?" Delacroix asked. "Who been hurt?"

"Everything's jake," I said. "Our new boy came in like a lion, but now he's passed out like a lamb. All's well that ends well."

"It ain't over yet," Delacroix said, looking up the Mile toward the cell where Wharton was jugged. *"L'homme mauvais, c'est vrai!"*

"Well," I said, "don't let it get you down, Del. Nobody's going to make you play skiprope with him out in the yard."

There was a creaking sound from behind me as Coffey got off his bunk. "Boss Edgecombe!" he said again. This time he sounded urgent. "I need to talk to you!"

I turned to him, thinking, all right, no problem, talking was my business. All the time trying not to shiver, because the fever had turned cold, as they sometimes will. Except for my groin, which still felt as if it had been slit open, filled with hot coals, and then sewed back up again.

"So talk, John Coffey," I said, trying to keep my voice light and calm. For the first time since he'd come onto E Block, Coffey looked as though he was really here, really among us. The almost ceaseless trickle of tears from the corners of his eyes *had* ceased, at least for the time being, and I knew he was seeing what he was looking at—Mr. Paul Edgecombe, E Block's bull-goose screw, and not some place he wished he could return to, and take back the terrible thing he'd done.

"No," he said. "You got to come in here."

"Now, you know I can't do that," I said, still trying for the light tone, "at least not right this minute. I'm on my own here for the time being, and you outweigh me by just about a ton and a half. We've had us one hooraw this afternoon, and that's enough. So we'll just have us a chat through the bars, if it's all the same to you, and—"

"Please!" He was holding the bars so tightly that his knuckles were pale and his fingernails were white. His face was long with distress, those strange eyes sharp with some need I could not understand. I remember thinking that maybe I *could've* understood it if I hadn't been so sick, and knowing that would have given me a way of helping him through the rest of it. When you know what a man needs, you know the man, more often than not. "Please, Boss Edgecombe! *You have to come in!*"

That's the nuttiest thing I ever heard, I thought, and then realized something even nuttier: I was going to do it. I had my keys off my belt and I was hunting through them for the ones that opened John Coffey's cell. He could have picked me up and broken me over his knee like kindling on a day when I was well and feeling fine, and this wasn't that day. All the same, I was going to do it. On my own, and less than half an hour after a graphic demonstration of where stupidity and laxness could get you when you were dealing with condemned murderers, I was going to open this black giant's cell, go in, and sit with him. If I was discovered, I might well lose my job even if he didn't do anything crazy, but I was going to do it, just the same.

Stop, I said to myself, you just stop now, Paul. But I didn't. I used one key on the top lock, another on the bottom lock, and then I slid the door back on its track.

"You know, boss, that maybe not such a good idear," Delacroix said in a voice so nervous and prissy it would probably have made me laugh under other circumstances.

"You mind your business and I'll mind mine," I said without looking around. My eyes were fixed on John Coffey's, and fixed so hard they might have been nailed there. It was like being hypnotized. My voice sounded to my own ears like something which had come echoing down a long valley. Hell, maybe I *was* hypnotized. "You just lie down and take you a rest."

"Christ, this place is crazy," Delacroix said in a trembling voice. "Mr. Jingles, I just about wish they'd fry me and be done widdit!"

I went into Coffey's cell. He stepped away as I stepped forward. When he was backed up against his bunk—it hit him in the calves, that's how tall he was—he sat down on it. He patted the mattress beside him, his eyes never once leaving mine. I sat down there next to him, and he put his arm around my shoulders, as if we were at the movies and I was his girl.

"What do you want, John Coffey?" I asked, still looking into his eyes—those sad, serene eyes.

"Just to help," he said. He sighed like a man will when he's faced with a job he doesn't much want to do, and then he put his hand down in my crotch, on that shelf of bone a foot or so below the navel.

"Hey!" I cried. "Get your goddam hand—"

A jolt slammed through me then, a big painless whack of something. It made me jerk on the cot and bow my back, made me think of Old Toot shouting that he was frying, he was frying, he was a done tom turkey. There was no heat, no feeling of electricity, but for a moment the color seemed to jump out of everything, as if the world had been somehow squeezed and made to sweat. I could see every pore on John Coffey's face, I could see every bloodshot snap in his haunted eyes, I could see a tiny healing scrape on his chin. I was aware that my fingers were hooked down into claws on thin air, and that my feet were drumming on the floor of Coffey's cell.

Then it was over. So was my urinary infection. Both the heat and the miserable throbbing pain were gone from my crotch, and the fever was likewise gone from my head. I could still feel the sweat it had drawn out of my skin, and I could smell it, but it was gone, all right.

"What's going on?" Delacroix called shrilly. His voice still came from far away, but when John Coffey bent forward, breaking eye-contact with me, the little Cajun's voice suddenly came clear. It was as if someone had pulled wads of cotton or a pair of shooters' plugs out of my ears. "What's he doing to you?"

I didn't answer. Coffey was bent forward over his own lap with his face working and his throat bulging. His eyes were bulging, too. He looked like a man with a chicken bone caught in his throat.

"John!" I said. I clapped him on the back; it was all I could think of to do. "John, what's wrong?"

He hitched under my hand, then made an unpleasant gagging, retching sound. His mouth opened the way horses sometimes open their mouths to allow the bit—reluctantly, with the lips peeling back from the teeth in a kind of desperate sneer. Then his teeth parted, too, and he exhaled a cloud of tiny black insects that looked like gnats or noseeums. They swirled furiously between his knees, turned white, and disappeared.

Suddenly all the strength went out of my midsection. It was as if the muscles there had turned to water. I slumped back against the stone side of Coffey's cell. I remember thinking the name of the Savior—Christ, Christ, Christ, over and over, like that—and I remember thinking that the fever had driven me delirious. That was all.

Then I became aware that Delacroix was bawling for help; he was telling the world that John Coffey was killing me, and telling it at the top of his lungs. Coffey was bending over me, all right, but only to make sure I was okay.

"Shut up, Del," I said, and got on my feet. I waited for the pain to rip into my guts, but it didn't happen. I was better. Really. There was a moment of dizziness, but that passed even before I was able to reach out and grab the bars of Coffey's cell door for balance. "I'm totally okey-doke."

"You get on outta dere," Delacroix said, sounding like a nervy old woman telling a kid to climb down out of that-ere apple tree. "You ain't suppose to be in there wit no one else on the block."

I looked at John Coffey, who sat on the bunk with his huge hands on the tree stumps of his knees. John Coffey looked back at me. He had to tilt his head up a little, but not much.

"What did you do, big boy?" I asked in a low voice. "What did you do to me?"

"Helped," he said. "I helped it, didn't I?"

"Yeah, I guess, but *how*? *How* did you help it?"

He shook his head—right, left, back to dead center. He didn't know how he'd helped it (how he'd *cured* it) and his placid face suggested that he didn't give a rat's ass—any more than I'd give a rat's ass about the mechanics of running when I was leading in the last fifty yards of a Fourth of July Two-Miler. I thought about asking him how he'd known I was sick in the first place, except that would undoubtedly have gotten the same headshake. There's a phrase I read somewhere and never forgot, something about "an enigma wrapped in a mystery." That's what John Coffey was, and I suppose the only reason he could sleep at night was because he didn't care. Percy called him the ijit, which was cruel but not too far off the mark. Our big boy knew his name, and knew it wasn't spelled like the drink, and that was just about all he cared to know.

As if to emphasize this for me, he shook his head in that deliberate way one more time, then lay down on his bunk with his hands clasped under his left cheek like a pillow and his face to the wall. His legs dangled off the end of the bunk from the shins on down, but that never seemed to bother him. The back of his shirt had pulled up, and I could see the scars that crisscrossed his skin.

I left the cell, turned the locks, then faced Delacroix, who was standing across the way with his hands wrapped around the bars of his cell, looking at me anxiously. Perhaps even fearfully. Mr. Jingles perched on his shoulder with his fine whiskers quivering like filaments. "What dat darkie-man do to you?" Delacroix asked. "Waddit gris-gris? He th'ow some gris-gris on you?" Spoken in that Cajun accent of his, *gris-gris* rhymed with *pee-pee*.

"I don't know what you're talking about, Del."

"Devil you don't! Lookit you! All change! Even walk different, boss!"

I probably *was* walking different, at that. There was a beautiful feeling of calm in my groin, a sense of peace so remarkable it was almost ecstasy—anyone who's suffered bad pain and then recovered will know what I'm talking about.

"Everything's all right, Del," I insisted. "John Coffey had a nightmare, that's all."

"He a gris-gris man!" Delacroix said vehemently. There was a nestle of sweat-beads on his upper lip. He hadn't seen much, just enough to scare him half to death. "He a hoodoo man!"

"What makes you say that?"

Delacroix reached up and took the mouse in one hand. He cupped it in his palm and lifted it to his face. From his pocket, Delacroix took out a pink fragment—one of those peppermint candies. He held it out, but at first the mouse ignored it, stretching out its neck toward the man instead, sniffing at his breath the way a person might sniff at a bouquet of flowers. Its little oildrop eyes slitted most of the way closed in an expression that looked like ecstasy. Delacroix kissed its nose, and the mouse allowed its nose to be kissed. Then it took the offered piece of candy and began to munch it. Delacroix looked at it a moment longer, then looked at me. All at once I got it.

"The mouse told you," I said. "Am I right?"

"*Oui.*"

"Like he whispered his name to you."

"*Oui*, in my ear he whisper it."

"Lie down, Del," I said. "Have you a little rest. All that whispering back and forth must wear you out."

He said something else—accused me of not believing

him, I suppose. His voice seemed to be coming from a long way off again. And when I went back up to the duty desk, I hardly seemed to be walking at all—it was more like I was floating, or maybe not even moving, the cells just rolling past me on either side, movie props on hidden wheels.

I started to sit like normal, but halfway into it my knees unlocked and I dropped onto the blue cushion Harry had brought from home the year before and plopped onto the seat of the chair. If the chair hadn't been there, I reckon I would have plopped straight to the floor without passing Go or collecting two hundred dollars.

I sat there, feeling the nothing in my groin where a forest fire had been blazing not ten minutes before. *I helped it, didn't I?* John Coffey had said, and that was true, as far as my body went. My peace of mind was a different story, though. *That* he hadn't helped at all.

My eyes fell on the stack of forms under the tin ashtray we kept on the corner of the desk. BLOCK REPORT was printed at the top, and about halfway down was a blank space headed *Report All Unusual Occurrences.* I would use that space in tonight's report, telling the story of William Wharton's colorful and action-packed arrival. But suppose I also told what had happened to me in John Coffey's cell? I saw myself picking up the pencil—the one whose tip Brutal was always licking—and writing a single word in big capital letters: MIRACLE.

That should have been funny, but instead of smiling, all at once I felt sure that I was going to cry. I put my hands to my face, palms against my mouth to stifle the sobs—I didn't want to scare Del again just when he was starting to get settled down—but no sobs came. No tears, either. After a few moments I lowered my hands back to the desk and folded them. I didn't know what I was feeling, and the only clear thought in my head was a wish that no one should come back onto the block until I was a little more in control of myself. I was afraid of what they might see in my face.

I drew a Block Report form toward me. I would wait until I had settled down a bit more to write about how my latest problem child had almost strangled Dean Stanton, but I could fill out the rest of the boilerplate foolishness in the meantime. I thought my handwriting might look funny—trembly—but it came out about the same as always.

About five minutes after I started, I put the pencil down and went into the W.C. adjacent to my office to take a leak. I didn't need to go very bad, but I could manage enough to test what had happened to me, I thought. As I stood there, waiting for my water to flow, I became sure that it would hurt just the way it had that morning, as if I were passing tiny shards of broken glass; what he'd done to me would turn out to be only hypnosis, after all, and that might be a relief in spite of the pain.

Except there was no pain, and what went into the bowl was clear, with no sign of pus. I buttoned my fly, pulled the chain that flushed the commode, went back to the duty desk, and sat down again.

I knew what had happened; I suppose I knew even when I was trying to tell myself I'd been hypnotized. I'd experienced a healing, an authentic Praise Jesus, The Lord Is Mighty. As a boy who'd grown up going to whatever Baptist or Pentecostal church my mother and her sisters happened to be in favor of during any given month, I had heard plenty of Praise Jesus, The Lord Is Mighty miracle stories. I didn't believe all of them, but there were plenty of people I did believe. One of these was a man named Roy Delfines, who lived with his family about two miles down the road from us when I was six or so. Delfines had chopped his son's little finger off with a hatchet, an accident which had occurred when the boy unexpectedly moved his hand on a log he'd been holding on the backyard chopping block for his dad. Roy Delfines said he had practically worn out the carpet with his knees that fall and winter, and in the spring the boy's finger had grown back. Even the nail had grown back. I believed Roy Delfines when he testified at Thursday-night rejoicing. There was a naked, uncomplicated honesty in what he said as he stood there talking with his hands jammed deep into the pockets of his biballs that was impossible *not* to believe. "It itch him some when thet finger started coming, kep him awake nights," Roy Delfines said, "but he knowed it was the Lord's itch and let it be." Praise Jesus, The Lord Is Mighty.

Roy Delfines's story was only one of many; I grew

up in a tradition of miracles and healings. I grew up believing in gris-gris, as well (only, up in the hills we said it to rhyme with *kiss-kiss*): stump-water for warts, moss under your pillow to ease the heartache of lost love, and, of course, what we used to call *haints*—but I did not believe John Coffey was a gris-gris man. I had looked into his eyes. More important, I had felt his touch. Being touched by him was like being touched by some strange and wonderful doctor.

I helped it, didn't I?

That kept chiming in my head, like a snatch of song you can't get rid of, or words you'd speak to set a spell.

I helped it, didn't I?

Except *he* hadn't. *God* had. John Coffey's use of "I" could be chalked up to ignorance rather than pride, but I knew—believed, at least—what I had learned about healing in those churches of Praise Jesus, The Lord Is Mighty, piney-woods amen corners much beloved by my twenty-two-year-old mother and my aunts: that healing is never about the healed or the healer, but about God's will. For one to rejoice at the sick made well is normal, quite the expected thing, but the person healed has an obligation to then ask why—to meditate on God's will, and the extraordinary lengths to which God has gone to realize His will.

What did God want of me, in this case? What did He want badly enough to put healing power in the hands of a child-murderer? To be on the block, instead of at home, sick as a dog, shivering in bed with the stink of sulfa running out of my pores? Perhaps; I was maybe supposed to be here instead of home in case Wild Bill Wharton decided to kick up more dickens, or to make sure Percy Wetmore didn't get up to some foolish and potentially destructive piece of fuckery. All right, then. So be it. I would keep my eyes open . . . and my mouth shut, especially about miracle cures.

No one was apt to question my looking and sounding better; I'd been telling the world I was getting better, and until that very day I'd honestly believed it. I had even told Warden Moores that I was on the mend. Delacroix had seen something, but I thought he would keep his mouth shut, too (probably afraid John Coffey would throw a spell on him if he didn't). As for Coffey himself, he'd probably already forgotten it. He was nothing but a conduit, after all, and there isn't a culvert in the world that remembers the water that flowed through it once the rain has stopped. So I resolved to keep my mouth completely shut on the subject, with never an idea of how soon I'd be telling the story, or who I'd be telling it to.

But I was curious about my big boy, and there's no sense not admitting it. After what had happened to me there in his cell, I was more curious than ever.

4

Before leaving that night, I arranged with Brutal to cover for me the next day, should I come in a little late, and when I got up the following morning, I set out for Tefton, down in Trapingus County.

"I'm not sure I like you worrying so much about this fellow Coffey," my wife said, handing me the lunch she'd put up for me—Janice never believed in roadside hamburger stands; she used to say there was a bellyache waiting in every one. "It's not like you, Paul."

"I'm not worried about him," I said. "I'm curious, that's all."

"In my experience, one leads to the other," Janice said tartly, then gave me a good, hearty kiss on the mouth. "You look better, at least, I'll say that. For awhile there, you had me nervous. Waterworks all cured up?"

"All cured up," I said, and off I went, singing songs like "Come, Josephine, in My Flying Machine" and "We're in the Money" to keep myself company.

I went to the offices of the Tefton *Intelligencer* first,

and they told me that Burt Hammersmith, the fellow I was looking for, was most likely over at the county courthouse. At the courthouse they told me that Hammersmith had been there but had left when a burst waterpipe had closed down the main proceedings, which happened to be a rape trial (in the pages of the *Intelligencer* the crime would be referred to as "assault on a woman," which was how such things were done in the days before Ricki Lake and Carnie Wilson came on the scene). They guessed he'd probably gone on home. I got some directions out a dirt road so rutted and narrow I just about didn't dare take my Ford up it, and there I found my man. Hammersmith had written most of the stories on the Coffey trial, and it was from him I found out most of the details about the brief manhunt that had netted Coffey in the first place. The details the *Intelligencer* considered too gruesome to print is what I mean, of course.

Mrs. Hammersmith was a young woman with a tired, pretty face and hands red from lye soap. She didn't ask my business, just led me through a small house fragrant with the smell of baking and onto the back porch, where her husband sat with a bottle of pop in his hand and an unopened copy of *Liberty* magazine on his lap. There was a small, sloping backyard; at the foot of it, two little ones were squabbling and laughing over a swing. From the porch, it was impossible to tell their sexes, but I thought they were boy and girl. Maybe even twins, which cast an interesting sort of light on their father's part, periph-

eral as it had been, in the Coffey trial. Nearer at
hand, set like an island in the middle of a turd-
studded patch of bare, beatup-looking ground, was a
doghouse. No sign of Fido; it was another unseasonably hot day, and I guessed he was probably inside,
snoozing.

"Burt, yew-all got you a cump'ny," Mrs. Hammersmith said.

"All right," he said. He glanced at me, glanced at
his wife, then looked back at his kids, which was
where his heart obviously lay. He was a thin man—
almost painfully thin, as if he had just begun to re-
cover from a serious illness—and his hair had started
to recede. His wife touched his shoulder tentatively
with one of her red, wash-swollen hands. He didn't
look at it or reach up to touch it, and after a moment
she took it back. It occurred to me, fleetingly, that
they looked more like brother and sister than husband and wife—he'd gotten the brains, she'd gotten
the looks, but neither of them had escaped some underlying resemblance, a heredity that could never be
escaped. Later, going home, I realized they didn't
look alike at all; what made them seem to was the
aftermath of stress and the lingering of sorrow. It's
strange how pain marks our faces, and makes us
look like family.

She said, "Yew-all want a cold drink, Mr.—?"

"It's Edgecombe," I said. "Paul Edgecombe. And
thank you. A cold drink would be wonderful,
ma'am."

She went back inside. I held out my hand to

Hammersmith, who gave it a brief shake. His grip was limp and cold. He never took his eyes off the kids down at the bottom of the yard.

"Mr. Hammersmith, I'm E Block superintendent at Cold Mountain State Prison. That's—"

"I know what it is," he said, looking at me with a little more interest. "So—the bull-goose screw of the Green Mile is standing on my back porch, just as big as life. What brings you fifty miles to talk to the local rag's only full-time reporter?"

"John Coffey," I said.

I think I expected some sort of strong reaction (the kids who could have been twins working at the back of my mind . . . and perhaps the doghouse, too; the Dettericks had had a dog), but Hammersmith only raised his eyebrows and sipped at his drink. "Coffey's *your* problem now, isn't he?" Hammersmith asked.

"He's not much of a problem," I said. "He doesn't like the dark, and he cries a lot of the time, but neither thing makes much of a problem in our line of work. We see worse."

"Cries a lot, does he?" Hammersmith asked. "Well, he's got a lot to cry about, I'd say. Considering what he did. What do you want to know?"

"Anything you can tell me. I've read your newspaper stories, so I guess what I want is anything that wasn't in them."

He gave me a sharp, dry look. "Like how the little girls looked? Like exactly what he did to them?

That the kind of stuff you're interested in, Mr. Edgecombe?"

"No," I said, keeping my voice mild. "It's not the Detterick girls I'm interested in, sir. Poor little mites are dead. But Coffey's not—not yet—and I'm curious about him."

"All right," he said. "Pull up a chair and sit, Mr. Edgecombe. You'll forgive me if I sounded a little sharp just now, but I get to see plenty of vultures in my line of work. Hell, I've been accused of being one of em often enough, myself. I just wanted to make sure of you."

"And are you?"

"Sure enough, I guess," he said, sounding almost indifferent. The story he told me is pretty much the one I set down earlier in this account—how Mrs. Detterick found the porch empty, with the screen door pulled off its upper hinge, the blankets cast into one corner, and blood on the steps; how her son and husband had taken after the girls' abductor; how the posse had caught up to them first and to John Coffey not much later. How Coffey had been sitting on the riverbank and wailing, with the bodies curled in his massive arms like big dolls. The reporter, rack-thin in his open-collared white shirt and gray town pants, spoke in a low, unemotional voice ... but his eyes never left his own two children as they squabbled and laughed and took turns with the swing down there in the shade at the foot of the slope. Sometime in the middle of the story, Mrs. Hammersmith came back with a bottle of homemade root beer, cold and strong and delicious. She stood listening for awhile, then interrupted long enough to call down to the kids and tell them to come up directly, she had cookies due out of the oven. "We will, Mamma!" called a little girl's voice, and the woman went back inside again.

When Hammersmith had finished, he said: "So why do you want to know? I never had me a visit from a Big House screw before, it's a first."

"I told you—"

"Curiosity, yep. Folks get curious, I know it, I even thank God for it, I'd be out of a job and might actually have to go to work for a living without it. But fifty miles is a long way to come to satisfy simple curiosity, especially when the last twenty is over bad roads. So why don't you tell me the truth, Edgecombe? I satisfied yours, so now you satisfy mine."

Well, I could say, *I had this urinary infection, and John Coffey put his hands on me and healed it. The man who raped and murdered those two little girls did that. So I wondered about him, of course—anyone would. I even wondered if maybe Homer Cribus and Deputy Rob McGee didn't maybe collar the wrong man. In spite of all the evidence against him I wonder that. Because a man who has a power like that in his hands, you don't usually think of him as the kind of man who rapes and murders children.*

No, maybe that wouldn't do.

"There are two things I've wondered about," I said. "The first is if he ever did anything like that before."

Hammersmith turned to me, his eyes suddenly sharp and bright with interest, and I saw he *was* a smart fellow. Maybe even a brilliant fellow, in a quiet way. "Why?" he asked. "What do you know, Edgecombe? What has he said?"

"Nothing. But a man who does this sort of thing once has usually done it before. They get a taste for it."

"Yes," he said. "They do. They certainly do."

"And it occurred to me that it would be easy enough to follow his backtrail and find out. A man his size, and a Negro to boot, can't be that hard to trace."

"You'd think so, but you'd be wrong," he said. "In Coffey's case, anyhow. I know."

"You tried?"

"I did, and came up all but empty. There were a couple of railroad fellows who thought they saw him in the Knoxville yards two days before the Detterick girls were killed. No surprise there; he was just across the river from the Great Southern tracks when they collared him, and that's probably how he came down here from Tennessee. I got a letter from a man who said he'd hired a big bald black man to shift crates for him in the early spring of this year—this was in Kentucky. I sent him a picture of Coffey and he said that was the man. But other than that—" Hammersmith shrugged and shook his head.

"Doesn't that strike you as a little odd?"

"Strikes me as a *lot* odd, Mr. Edgecombe. It's like

he dropped out of the sky. And he's no help; he can't remember last week once this week comes."

"No, he can't," I said. "How do you explain it?"

"We're in a Depression," he said, "*that's* how I explain it. People all over the roads. The Okies want to pick peaches in California, the poor whites from up in the brakes want to build cars in Detroit, the black folks from Mississippi want to go up to New England and work in the shoe factories or the textile mills. Everyone—black as well as white—thinks it's going to be better over the next jump of land. It's the American damn way. Even a giant like Coffey doesn't get noticed everywhere he goes . . . until, that is, he decides to kill a couple of little girls. Little *white* girls."

"Do you believe that?" I asked.

He gave me a bland look from his too-thin face. "Sometimes I do," he said.

His wife leaned out of the kitchen window like an engineer from the cab of a locomotive and called, "*Kids! Cookies are ready!*" She turned to me. "Would you like an oatmeal-raisin cookie, Mr. Edgecombe?"

"I'm sure they're delicious, ma'am, but I'll take a pass this time."

"All right," she said, and drew her head back inside.

"Have you seen the scars on him?" Hammersmith asked abruptly. He was still watching his kids, who couldn't quite bring themselves to abandon the pleasures of the swing—not even for oatmeal-raisin cookies.

"Yes." But I was surprised he had.

He saw my reaction and laughed. "The defense attorney's one big victory was getting Coffey to take off his shirt and show those scars to the jury. The prosecutor, George Peterson, objected like hell, but the judge allowed it. Old George could have saved his breath—juries around these parts don't buy all that psychology crap about how people who've been mistreated just can't help themselves. They believe people *can* help themselves. It's a point of view I have a lot of sympathy for . . . but those scars were pretty ghastly, just the same. Notice anything about them, Edgecombe?"

I had seen the man naked in the shower, and I'd noticed, all right; I knew just what he was talking about. "They're all broken up. Latticed, almost."

"You know what that means?"

"Somebody whopped the living hell out of him when he was a kid," I said. "Before he grew."

"But they didn't manage to whop the devil out of him, did they, Edgecombe? Should have spared the rod and just drowned him in the river like a stray kitten, don't you think?"

I suppose it would have been politic to simply agree and get out of there, but I couldn't. I'd seen him. And I'd *felt* him, as well. Felt the touch of his hands.

"He's . . . strange," I said. "But there doesn't seem to be any real violence in him. I know how he was found, and it's hard to jibe that with what I see, day in and day out, on the block. I know violent men, Mr.

Hammersmith." It was Wharton I was thinking about, of course, Wharton strangling Dean Stanton with his wrist-chain and bellowing *Whoooee, boys! Ain't this a party, now?*

He was looking at me closely now, and smiling a little, incredulous smile that I didn't care for very much. "You didn't come up here to get an idea about whether or not he might have killed some other little girls somewhere else," he said. "You came up here to see if I think he did it at all. That's it, isn't it? 'Fess up, Edgecombe."

I swallowed the last of my cold drink, put the bottle down on the little table, and said: "Well? Do you?"

"Kids!" he called down the hill, leaning forward a little in his chair to do it. *"Y'all come on up here now n get your cookies!"* Then he leaned back in his chair again and looked at me. That little smile—the one I didn't much care for—had reappeared.

"Tell you something," he said. "You want to listen close, too, because this might just be something you need to know."

"I'm listening."

"We had us a dog named Sir Galahad," he said, and cocked a thumb at the doghouse. "A good dog. No particular breed, but gentle. Calm. Ready to lick your hand or fetch a stick. There are plenty of mongrel dogs like him, wouldn't you say?"

I shrugged, nodded.

"In many ways, a good mongrel dog is like your negro," he said. "You get to know it, and often you grow to love it. It is of no particular use, but you keep it around because you *think* it loves *you*. If you're lucky, Mr. Edgecombe, you never have to find out any different. Cynthia and I, we were not lucky." He sighed—a long and somehow skeletal sound, like the wind rummaging through fallen leaves. He pointed toward the doghouse again, and I wondered how I had missed its general air of abandonment earlier, or the fact that many of the turds had grown whitish and powdery at their tops.

"I used to clean up after him," Hammersmith said, "and keep the roof of his house repaired against the rain. In that way also Sir Galahad was like your Southern negro, who will not do those things for himself. Now I don't touch it, I haven't been near it since the accident . . . if you can call it an accident. I went over there with my rifle and shot him, but I haven't been over there since. I can't bring myself to. I suppose I will, in time. I'll clean up his messes and tear down his house."

Here came the kids, and all at once I didn't want them to come; all at once that was the last thing on earth I wanted. The little girl was all right, but the boy—

They pounded up the steps, looked at me, giggled, then went on toward the kitchen door.

"Caleb," Hammersmith said. "Come here. Just for a second."

The little girl—surely his twin, they had to be of an age—went on into the kitchen. The little boy came to his father, looking down at his feet. He knew he was ugly. He was only four, I guess, but four is old enough to know that you're ugly. His father put two fingers under the boy's chin and tried to raise his face. At first the boy resisted, but when his father said "Please, son," in tones of sweetness and calmness and love, he did as he was asked.

A huge, circular scar ran out of his hair, down his forehead, through one dead and indifferently cocked eye, and to the corner of his mouth, which had been disfigured into the knowing leer of a gambler or perhaps a whoremaster. One cheek was smooth and pretty; the other was bunched up like the stump of a tree. I guessed there had been a hole in it, but that, at least, had healed.

"He has the one eye," Hammersmith said, caressing the boy's bunched cheek with a lover's kind fingers. "I suppose he's lucky not to be blind. We get down on our knees and thank God for that much, at least. Eh, Caleb?"

"Yes, sir," the boy said shyly—the boy who would be beaten mercilessly on the play-yard by laughing, jeering bullies for all his miserable years of education, the boy who would never be asked to play Spin the Bottle or Post Office and would probably never sleep with a woman not bought and paid for once he was grown to manhood's times and needs, the boy who would always stand outside the warm and lighted circle of his peers, the boy who would look at himself in his mirror for the next fifty or sixty or seventy years of his life and think *ugly, ugly, ugly.*

"Go on in and get your cookies," his father said, and kissed his son's sneering mouth.

"Yes, sir," Caleb said, and dashed inside.

Hammersmith took a handkerchief from his back pocket and wiped at his eyes with it—they were dry, but I suppose he'd gotten used to them being wet.

"The dog was here when they were born," he said. "I brought him in the house to smell them when Cynthia brought them home from the hospital, and Sir Galahad licked their hands. Their little hands." He nodded, as if confirming this to himself. "He played with them; used to lick Arden's face until she giggled. Caleb used to pull his ears, and when he was first learning to walk, he'd sometimes go around the yard, holding to Galahad's tail. The dog never so much as *growled* at him. Either of them."

Now the tears were coming; he wiped at them automatically, as a man does when he's had lots of practice.

"There was no reason," he said. "Caleb didn't hurt him, yell at him, anything. I know. I was there. If I hadn't have been, the boy would almost certainly have been killed. What happened, Mr. Edgecombe, was *nothing*. The boy just got his face set the right way in front of the dog's face, and it came into Sir Galahad's mind—whatever serves a dog for a mind—to lunge and bite. To kill, if he could. The boy was there in front of him and the dog bit. And that's what happened with Coffey. He was there, he saw them on the porch, he took them, he raped them, he killed them. You say there should be some hint that he did something like it before, and I know what you mean, but maybe he *didn't* do it before. My dog never bit before; just that once. Maybe, if Coffey was let go, he'd never do it again. Maybe my dog never would have bit again. But I didn't concern myself with that, you know. I went out with my rifle and grabbed his collar and blew his head off."

He was breathing hard.

"I'm as enlightened as the next man, Mr. Edge-combe, went to college in Bowling Green, took history as well as journalism, some philosophy, too. I like to think of myself as enlightened. I don't suppose folks up North would, but I like to think of myself as enlightened. I'd not bring slavery back for all the tea in China. I think we have to be humane and generous in our efforts to solve the race problem. But we have to remember that your negro will bite if he gets the chance, just like a mongrel dog will bite if he gets the chance and it crosses his mind to do so. You want to know if he did it, your weepy Mr. Coffey with the scars all over him?"

I nodded.

"Oh, yes," Hammersmith said. "He did it. Don't you doubt it, and don't you turn your back on him. You might get away with it once or a hundred times ... even a thousand ... but in the end—" He raised a hand before my eyes and snapped the fingers together rapidly against the thumb, turning the hand into a biting mouth. "You understand?"

I nodded again.

"He raped them, he killed them, and afterward he

was sorry . . . but those little girls stayed raped, those little girls stayed dead. But you'll fix him, won't you, Edgecombe? In a few weeks you'll fix him so he never does anything like that again." He got up, went to the porch rail, and looked vaguely at the doghouse, standing at the center of its beaten patch, in the middle of those aging turds. "Perhaps you'll excuse me," he said. "Since I don't have to spend the afternoon in court, I thought I might visit with my family for a little bit. A man's children are only young once."

"You go ahead," I said. My lips felt numb and distant. "And thank you for your time."

"Don't mention it," he said.

I drove directly from Hammersmith's house to the prison. It was a long drive, and this time I wasn't able to shorten it by singing songs. It felt like all the songs had gone out of me, at least for awhile. I kept seeing that poor little boy's disfigured face. And Hammersmith's hand, the fingers going up and down against the thumb in a biting motion.

5

Wild Bill Wharton took his first trip down to the restraint room the very next day. He spent the morning and afternoon being as quiet and good as Mary's little lamb, a state we soon discovered was not natural to him, and meant trouble. Then, around seven-thirty that evening, Harry felt something warm splash on the cuffs of uniform pants he had put on clean just that day. It was piss. William Wharton was standing at his cell, showing his darkening teeth in a wide grin, and pissing all over Harry Terwilliger's pants and shoes.

"The dirty sonofabitch must have been saving it up all day," Harry said later, still disgusted and outraged.

Well, that was it. It was time to show William Wharton who ran the show on E Block. Harry got Brutal and me, and I alerted Dean and Percy, who were also on. We had three prisoners by then, remember, and were into what we called full coverage, with my group on from seven in the evening to three in the morning—when trouble was most apt to break out—and two other crews covering the rest of the day. Those other crews consisted mostly of floaters, with Bill Dodge usually in charge. It wasn't a bad way to run things, all and all, and I felt that, once I could shift Percy over to days, life would be even better. I never got around to that, however. I sometimes wonder if it would have changed things, if I had.

Anyway, there was a big watermain in the storage room, on the side away from Old Sparky, and Dean and Percy hooked up a length of canvas firehose to it. Then they stood by the valve that would open it, if needed.

Brutal and I hurried down to Wharton's cell, where Wharton still stood, still grinning and still with his tool hanging out of his pants. I had liberated the straitjacket from the restraint room and tossed it on a shelf in my office last thing before going home the night before, thinking we might be needing it for our new problem child. Now I had it in one hand, my index finger hooked under one of the canvas straps. Harry came behind us, hauling the nozzle of the firehose, which ran back through my office, down the storage-room steps, and to the drum where Dean and Percy were paying it out as fast as they could.

"Hey, d'jall like that?" Wild Bill asked. He was laughing like a kid at a carnival, laughing so hard he could barely talk; big tears went rolling down his cheeks. "You come on s'fast I guess you must've. I'm currently cookin some turds to go with it. Nice soft ones. I'll have them out to y'all tomorrow—"

He saw that I was unlocking his cell door and his eyes narrowed. He saw that Brutal was holding his revolver in one hand and his nightstick in the other, and they narrowed even more.

"You can come in here on your legs, but you'll go out on your backs, Billy the Kid is goan guarantee you that," he told us. His eyes shifted back to me. "And if you think you're gonna put that nut-coat on me, you got another think coming, old hoss."

"You're not the one who says go or jump back around here," I told him. "You should know that, but I guess you're too dumb to pick it up without a little teaching."

I finished unlocking the door and ran it back on its track. Wharton retreated to the bunk, his cock still hanging out of his pants, put his hands out to me, palms up, then beckoned with his fingers. "Come on, you ugly motherfucker," he said. "They be schoolin, all right, but this old boy's well set up to be the teacher." He shifted his gaze and his dark-toothed grin to Brutal. "Come on, big fella, you first. This time you cain't sneak up behind me. Put down that gun—you ain't gonna shoot it anyway, not you—and we'll go man-to-man. See who's the better fel—"

Brutal stepped into the cell, but not toward Wharton. He moved to the left once he was through the door, and Wharton's narrow eyes widened as he saw the firehose pointed at him.

"No, you don't," he said. "Oh no, you d—"

"*Dean!*" I yelled. "*Turn it on! All the way!*"

Wharton jumped forward, and Brutal hit him a good smart lick—the kind of lick I'm sure Percy dreamed of—across his forehead, laying his baton right over Wharton's eyebrows. Wharton, who seemed to think we'd never seen trouble until we'd seen him, went to his knees, his eyes open but blind. Then the water came, Harry staggering back a step under its power and then holding steady, the nozzle firm in his hands, pointed like a gun. The stream caught Wild Bill Wharton square in the middle of his chest, spun him halfway around, and drove him back under his bunk. Down the hall, Delacroix was jumping from foot to foot, cackling shrilly, and cursing at John Coffey, demanding that Coffey tell him what was going on, who was winning, and how dat *gran' fou* new boy like dat Chinee water treatment. John said nothing, just stood there quietly in his too-short pants and his prison slippers. I only had one quick glance at him, but that was enough to observe his same old expression, both sad and serene. It was as if he'd seen the whole thing before, not just once or twice but a thousand times.

"Kill the water!" Brutal shouted back over his shoulder, then raced forward into the cell. He sank his hands into the semi-conscious Wharton's armpits and dragged him out from under his bunk. Wharton was coughing and making a glub-glub sound. Blood was dribbling into his dazed eyes from above his brows, where Brutal's stick had popped the skin open in a line.

We had the straitjacket business down to a science,

did Brutus Howell and me; we'd practiced it like a couple of vaudeville hoofers working up a new dance routine. Every now and then, that practice paid off. Now, for instance. Brutal sat Wharton up and held out his arms toward me the way a kid might hold out the arms of a Raggedy Andy doll. Awareness was just starting to seep back into Wharton's eyes, the knowledge that if he didn't start fighting right away, it was going to be too late, but the lines were still down between his brain and his muscles, and before he could repair them, I had rammed the sleeves of the coat up his arms and Brutal was doing the buckles up the back. While he took care of that, I grabbed the cuff-straps, pulled Wharton's arms around his sides, and linked his wrists together with another canvas strap. He ended up looking like he was hugging himself.

"Goddam you, big dummy, how dey doin widdim?" Delacroix screamed. I heard Mr. Jingles squeaking, as if he wanted to know, too.

Percy arrived, his shirt wet and sticking to him from his struggles with the watermain, his face glowing with excitement. Dean came along behind him, wearing a bracelet of purplish bruise around his throat and looking a lot less thrilled.

"Come on, now, Wild Bill," I said, and yanked Wharton to his feet. "Little walky-walky."

"Don't you call me that!" Wharton screamed shrilly, and I think that for the first time we were seeing real feelings, and not just a clever animal's camouflage spots. "Wild Bill Hickok wasn't no range-rider! He

never fought him no bear with a Bowie knife, either! He was just another bushwhackin John Law! Dumb sonofabitch sat with his back to the door and got kilt by a drunk!"

"Oh my suds and body, a *history lesson*!" Brutal exclaimed, and shoved Wharton out of his cell. "A feller just never knows what he's going to get when he clocks in here, only that it's apt to be nice. But with so many nice people like you around, I guess that kind of stands to reason, don't it? And you know what? Pretty soon you'll be history yourself, Wild Bill. Meantime, you get on down the hall. We got a room for you. Kind of a cooling-off room."

Wharton gave a furious, inarticulate scream and threw himself at Brutal, even though he was snugly buckled into the coat now, and his arms were wrapped around behind him. Percy made to draw his baton—the Wetmore Solution for all of life's problems—and Dean put a hand on his wrist. Percy gave him a puzzled, half-indignant look, as if to say that after what Wharton had done to Dean, Dean should be the last person in the world to want to hold him back.

Brutal pushed Wharton backward. I caught him and pushed him to Harry. And Harry propelled him on down the Green Mile, past the gleeful Delacroix and the impassive Coffey. Wharton ran to keep from falling on his face, spitting curses the whole way. Spitting them the way a welder's torch spits sparks. We banged him into the last cell on the right while Dean, Harry, and Percy (who for once wasn't complaining about being unfairly overworked) yanked all of the crap out of the restraint room. While they did that, I had a brief conversation with Wharton.

"You think you're tough," I said, "and maybe you are, sonny, but in here tough don't matter. Your stampeding days are over. If you take it easy on us, we'll take it easy on you. If you make it hard, you'll die in the end just the same, only we'll sharpen you like a pencil before you go."

"You're gonna be so happy to see the end of me," Wharton said in a hoarse voice. He was struggling against the straitjacket even though he must have known it would do no good, and his face was as red as a tomato. "And until I'm gone, I'll make your lives miserable." He bared his teeth at me like an angry baboon.

"If that's all you want, to make our lives miserable, you can quit now, because you've already succeeded," Brutal said. "But as far as your time on the Mile goes, Wharton, we don't care if you spend all of it in the room with the soft walls. And you can wear that damned nut-coat until your arms gangrene from lack of circulation and fall right off." He paused. "No one much comes down here, you know. And if you think anyone gives much of a shit what happens to you, one way or another, you best reconsider. To the world in general, you're already one dead outlaw."

Wharton was studying Brutal carefully, and the choler was fading out of his face. "Lemme out of it," he said in a placatory voice—a voice too sane and too reasonable to trust. "I'll be good. Honest Injun."

Harry appeared in the cell doorway. The end of the corridor looked like a rummage sale, but we'd set things to rights with good speed once we got started. We had before; we knew the drill. "All ready," Harry said.

Brutal grabbed the bulge in the canvas where Wharton's right elbow was and yanked him to his feet. "Come on, Wild Billy. And look on the good side. You're gonna have at least twenty-four hours to remind yourself never to sit with your back to the door, and to never hold onto no aces and eights."

"Lemme out of it," Wharton said. He looked from Brutal to Harry to me, the red creeping back into his face. "I'll be good—I tell you I've learned my lesson. I . . . I . . . *ummmmmahhhhhhh—*"

He suddenly collapsed, half of him in the cell, half of him on the played-out lino of the Green Mile, kicking his feet and bucking his body.

"Holy Christ, he's pitchin a fit," Percy whispered.

"Sure, and my sister's the Whore of Babylon," Brutal said. "She dances the hootchie-kootchie for Moses on Saturday nights in a long white veil." He bent down and hooked a hand into one of Wharton's armpits. I got the other one. Wharton threshed between us like a hooked fish. Carrying his jerking body, listening to him grunt from one end and fart from the other was one of my life's less pleasant experiences.

I looked up and met John Coffey's eyes for a second. They were bloodshot, and his dark cheeks were wet. He had been crying again. I thought of Hammersmith making that biting gesture with his hand and shivered a little. Then I turned my attention back to Wharton.

We threw him into the restraint room like he was cargo, and watched him lie on the floor, bucking hard in the straitjacket next to the drain we had once checked for the mouse which had started its E Block life as Steamboat Willy.

"I don't much care if he swallows his tongue or something and dies," Dean said in his hoarse and raspy voice, "but think of the paperwork, boys! It'd never end."

"Never mind the paperwork, think of the hearing," Harry said gloomily. "We'd lose our damned jobs. End up picking peas down Mississippi. You know what Mississippi is, don't you? It's the Indian word for asshole."

"He ain't gonna die, and he ain't gonna swallow his tongue, either," Brutal said. "When we open this door tomorrow, he's gonna be just fine. Take my word for it."

That's the way it was, too. The man we took back to his cell the next night at nine was quiet, pallid, and seemingly chastened. He walked with his head down, made no effort to attack anyone when the straitjacket came off, and only stared listlessly at me when I told him it would go just the same the next time, and he just had to ask himself how much time he wanted to spend pissing in his pants and eating baby-food a spoonful at a time.

"I'll be good, boss, I learnt my lesson," he whispered in a humble little voice as we put him back in his cell. Brutal looked at me and winked.

Late the next day, William Wharton, who was Billy the Kid to himself and never that bushwhacking John Law Wild Bill Hickok, bought a moon-pie from Old Toot-Toot. Wharton had been expressly forbidden any such commerce, but the afternoon crew was composed of floaters, as I think I have said, and the deal went down. Toot himself undoubtedly knew better, but to him the snack-wagon was always a case of a nickel is a nickel, a dime is a dime, I'd sing another chorus but I don't have the time.

That night, when Brutal ran his check-round, Wharton was standing at the door of his cell. He waited until Brutal looked up at him, then slammed the heels of his hands into his bulging cheeks and shot a thick and amazingly long stream of chocolate sludge into Brutal's face. He had crammed the entire moon-pie into his trap, held it there until it liquefied, and then used it like chewing tobacco.

Wharton fell back on his bunk wearing a chocolate goatee, kicking his legs and screaming with laughter and pointing to Brutal, who was wearing a lot more than a goatee. "Li'l Black Sambo, yassuh, hoos, yassuh, how*doo* you do?" Wharton held his belly and howled. "Gosh, if it had only been ka-ka! I wish it had been! If I'd had me some of that—"

"You *are* ka-ka," Brutal growled, "and I hope you got your bags packed, because you're going back down to your favorite toilet."

Once again Wharton was bundled into the straitjacket, and once again we stowed him in the room with the soft walls. Two days, this time. Sometimes we could hear him raving in there, sometimes we could hear him promising that he'd be good, that he'd come to his senses and be good, and sometimes we could hear him screaming that he needed a doctor, that he was dying. Mostly, though, he was silent. And he was silent when we took him out again, too, walking back to his cell with his head down and his eyes dull, not responding when Harry said, "Remember, it's up to you." He would be all right for a while, and then he'd try something else. There was nothing he did that hadn't been tried before (well, except for the thing with the moon-pie, maybe; even Brutal admitted that was pretty original), but his sheer persistence was scary. I was afraid that sooner or later someone's attention might lapse and there would be hell to pay. And the situation might continue for quite awhile, because somewhere he had a lawyer who was beating the bushes, telling folks how wrong it would be to kill this fellow upon whose brow the dew of youth had not yet dried . . . and who was, incidentally, as white as old Jeff Davis. There was no sense complaining about it, because keeping Wharton out of the chair was his lawyer's job. Keeping him safely jugged was ours. And in the end, Old Sparky would almost certainly have him, lawyer or no lawyer.

6

That was the week Melinda Moores, the warden's wife, came home from Indianola. The doctors were done with her; they had their interesting, new-fangled X-ray photographs of the tumor in her head; they had documented the weakness in her hand and the paralyzing pains that racked her almost constantly by then, and were done with her. They gave her husband a bunch of pills with morphine in them and sent Melinda home to die. Hal Moores had some sick-leave piled up—not a lot, they didn't give you a lot in those days, but he took what he had so he could help her do what she had to do.

My wife and I went to see her three days or so after she came home. I called ahead and Hal said yes, that would be fine, Melinda was having a pretty good day and would enjoy seeing us.

"I hate calls like this," I said to Janice as we drove to the little house where the Mooreses had spent most of their marriage.

"So does everyone, honey," she said, and patted my hand. "We'll bear up under it, and so will she."

"I hope so."

We found Melinda in the sitting room, planted in a bright slant of unseasonably warm October sun, and my first shocked thought was that she had lost ninety pounds. She hadn't, of course—if she'd lost that much weight, she hardly would have been there at all—but that was my brain's initial reaction to what my eyes were reporting. Her face had fallen away to show the shape of the underlying skull, and her skin was as white as parchment. There were dark circles under her eyes. And it was the first time I ever saw her in her rocker when she didn't have a lapful of sewing or afghan squares or rags for braiding into a rug. She was just sitting there. Like a person in a train-station.

"Melinda," my wife said warmly. I think she was as shocked as I was—more, perhaps—but she hid it splendidly, as some women seem able to do. She went to Melinda, dropped on one knee beside the rocking chair in which the warden's wife sat, and took one of her hands. As she did, my eye happened on the blue hearthrug by the fireplace. It occurred to me that it should have been the shade of tired old limes, because now this room was just another version of the Green Mile.

"I brought you some tea," Jan said, "the kind I put up myself. It's a nice sleepy tea. I've left it in the kitchen."

"Thank you so much, darlin," Melinda said. Her voice sounded old and rusty.

"How you feeling, dear?" my wife asked.

"Better," Melinda said in her rusty, grating voice. "Not so's I want to go out to a barn dance, but at least there's no pain today. They give me some pills for the headaches. Sometimes they even work."

"That's good, isn't it?"

"But I can't grip so well. Something's happened . . . to my hand." She raised it, looked at it as if she had never seen it before, then lowered it back into her lap. "Something's happened . . . all over me." She began to cry in a soundless way that made me think of John Coffey. It started to chime in my head again, that thing he'd said: *I helped it, didn't I? I helped it, didn't I?* Like a rhyme you can't get rid of.

Hal came in then. He collared me, and you can believe me when I say I was glad to be collared. We went into the kitchen, and he poured me half a shot of white whiskey, hot stuff fresh out of some countryman's still. We clinked our glasses together and drank. The shine went down like coal-oil, but the bloom in the belly was heaven. Still, when Moores tipped the mason jar at me, wordlessly asking if I wanted the other half, I shook my head and waved it off. Wild Bill Wharton was out of restraints—for the time being, anyway—and it wouldn't be safe to go near where he was with a booze-clouded head. Not even with bars between us.

"I don't know how long I can take this, Paul," he said in a low voice. "There's a girl who comes in mornings to help me with her, but the doctors say she may lose control of her bowels, and . . . and . . ."

He stopped, his throat working, trying hard not to cry in front of me again.

"Go with it as best you can," I said. I reached out across the table and briefly squeezed his palsied, liverspotted hand. "Do that day by day and give the rest over to God. There's nothing else you can do, is there?"

"I guess not. But it's hard, Paul. I pray you never have to find out how hard."

He made an effort to collect himself.

"Now tell me the news. How are you doing with William Wharton? And how are you making out with Percy Wetmore?"

We talked shop for a while, and got through the visit. After, all the way home, with my wife sitting silent, for the most part—wet-eyed and thoughtful—in the passenger seat beside me, Coffey's words ran around in my head like Mr. Jingles running around in Delacroix's cell: *I helped it, didn't I?*

"It's terrible," my wife said dully at one point. "And there's nothing anyone can do to help her."

I nodded agreement and thought, *I helped it, didn't I?* But that was crazy, and I tried as best I could to put it out of my mind.

As we turned into our dooryard, she finally spoke a second time—not about her old friend Melinda, but about my urinary infection. She wanted to know if it was really gone. Really gone, I told her.

"That's fine, then," she said, and kissed me over the eyebrow, in that shivery place of mine. "Maybe we ought to, you know, get up to a little something. If you have the time and the inclination, that is."

Having plenty of the latter and just enough of the former, I took her by the hand and led her into the back bedroom and took her clothes off as she stroked the part of me that swelled and throbbed but didn't hurt anymore. And as I moved in her sweetness, slipping through it in that slow way she liked—that we both liked—I thought of John Coffey, saying he'd helped it, he'd helped it, hadn't he? Like a snatch of song that won't leave your mind until it's damned good and ready.

Later, as I drove to the prison, I got to thinking that very soon we would have to start rehearsing for Delacroix's execution. That thought led to how Percy was going to be out front this time, and I felt a shiver of dread. I told myself to just go with it, one execution and we'd very likely be shut of Percy Wetmore for good . . . but still I felt that shiver, as if the infection I'd been suffering with wasn't gone at all, but had only switched locations, from boiling my groin to freezing my backbone.

7

"Come on," Brutal told Delacroix the following evening. "We're going for a little walk. You and me and Mr. Jingles."

Delacroix looked at him distrustfully, then reached down into the cigar box for the mouse. He cupped it in the palm of one hand and looked at Brutal with narrowed eyes.

"Whatchoo talking about?" he asked.

"It's a big night for you and Mr. Jingles," Dean said, as he and Harry joined Brutal. The chain of bruises around Dean's neck had gone an unpleasant yellow color, but at least he could talk again without sounding like a dog barking at a cat. He looked at Brutal. "Think we ought to put the shackles on him, Brute?"

Brutal appeared to consider. "Naw," he said at last. "He's gonna be good, ain't you, Del? You and the mouse, both. After all, you're gonna be showin off for some high muck-a-mucks tonight."

Percy and I were standing up by the duty desk, watching this, Percy with his arms folded and a small, contemptuous smile on his lips. After a bit, he took out his horn comb and went to work on his hair with it. John Coffey was watching, too, standing silently at the bars of his cell. Wharton was lying on his bunk, staring up at the ceiling and ignoring the whole show. He was still "being good," although what he called *good* was what the docs at Briar Ridge called *catatonic*. And there was one other person there, as well. He was tucked out of sight in my office, but his skinny shadow fell out the door and onto the Green Mile.

"What dis about, you *gran' fou*?" Del asked querulously, drawing his feet up on the bunk as Brutal undid the double locks on his cell door and ran it open. His eyes flicked back and forth among the three of them.

"Well, I tell you," Brutal said. "Mr. Moores is gone for awhile—his wife is under the weather, as you may have heard. So Mr. Anderson is in charge, Mr. Curtis Anderson."

"Yeah? What that got to do with me?"

"Well," Harry said, "Boss Anderson's heard about your mouse, Del, and wants to see him perform. He and about six other fellows are over in Admin, just waiting for you to show up. Not just plain old bluesuit guards, either. These are pretty big bugs, just like Brute said. One of them, I believe, is a politician all the way from the state capital."

Delacroix swelled visibly at this, and I saw not so much as a single shred of doubt on his face. Of *course* they wanted to see Mr. Jingles; who would not?

He scrummed around, first under his bunk and then under his pillow. He eventually found one of those big pink peppermints and the wildly colored spool. He looked at Brutal questioningly, and Brutal nodded.

"Yep. It's the spool trick they're really wild to see, I guess, but the way he eats those mints is pretty damned cute, too. And don't forget the cigar box. You'll want it to carry him in, right?"

Delacroix got the box and put Mr. Jingles's props in it, but mouse he settled on the shoulder of his shirt. Then he stepped out of his cell, his puffed-out chest leading the way, and regarded Dean and Harry. "You boys coming?"

"Naw," Dean said. "Got other fish to fry. But you knock em for a loop, Del—show em what happens when a Louisiana boy puts the hammer down and really goes to work."

"You bet." A smile shone out of his face, so sudden and so simple in its happiness that I felt my heart break for him a little, in spite of the terrible thing he had done. What a world we live in—what a world!

Delacroix turned to John Coffey, with whom he had struck up a diffident friendship not much different from a hundred other deathhouse acquaintances I'd seen.

"You knock em for a loop, Del," Coffey said in a serious voice. "You show em all his tricks."

Delacroix nodded and held his hand up by his shoulder. Mr. Jingles stepped onto it like it was a platform, and Delacroix held the hand out toward

Coffey's cell. John Coffey stuck out a huge finger, and I'll be damned if that mouse didn't stretch out his neck and lick the end of it, just like a dog.

"Come on, Del, quit lingerin," Brutal said. "These folks're settin back a hot dinner at home to watch your mouse cut his capers." Not true, of course—Anderson would have been there until eight o'clock on any night, and the guards he'd dragged in to watch Delacroix's "show" would be there until eleven or twelve, depending on when their shifts were scheduled to end. The politician from the state capital would most likely turn out to be an office janitor in a borrowed tie. But Delacroix had no way of knowing any of that.

"I'm ready," Delacroix said, speaking with the simplicity of a great star who has somehow managed to retain the common touch. "Let's go." And as Brutal led him up the Green Mile with Mr. Jingles perched there on the little man's shoulder, Delacroix once more began to bugle, *"Messieurs et mesdames! Bienvenue au cirque de mousie!"* Yet, even lost as deeply in his own fantasy world as he was, he gave Percy a wide berth and a mistrustful glance.

Harry and Dean stopped in front of the empty cell across from Wharton's (that worthy had still not so much as stirred). They watched as Brutal unlocked the door to the exercise yard, where another two guards were waiting to join him, and led Delacroix out, bound for his command performance before the grand high poohbahs of Cold Mountain Penitentiary. We waited until the door was locked again, and then

I looked toward my office. That shadow was still lying on the floor, thin as famine, and I was glad Delacroix had been too excited to see it.

"Come on out," I said. "And let's move along brisk, folks. I want to get two run-throughs in, and we don't have much time."

Old Toot-Toot, looking as bright-eyed and bushytailed as ever, came out, walked to Delacroix's cell, and strolled in through the open door. "Sittin down," he said. "I'm sittin down, I'm sittin down, I'm sittin down."

This is the real circus, I thought, closing my eyes for a second. This is the real circus right here, and we're all just a bunch of trained mice. Then I put the thought out of my mind, and we started to rehearse.

8

The first rehearsal went well, and so did the second. Percy performed better than I could have hoped for in my wildest dreams. That didn't mean things would go right when the time really came for the Cajun to walk the Mile, but it was a big step in the right direction. It occurred to me that it had gone well because Percy was at long last doing something he cared about. I felt a surge of contempt at that, and pushed it away. What did it matter? He would cap Delacroix and roll him, and then both of them would be gone. If that wasn't a happy ending, what was? And, as Moores had pointed out, Delacroix's nuts were going to fry no matter who was out front.

Still, Percy had shown to good advantage in his new role and he knew it. We all did. As for me, I was too relieved to dislike him much, at least for the time being. It looked as if things were going to go all right. I was further relieved to find that Percy actually listened when we suggested some things he could do that might improve his performance even more, or at least cut down the possibility of something going wrong. If you want to know the truth, we got pretty enthusiastic about it—even Dean, who ordinarily stood well back from Percy . . . physically as well as mentally, if he could. None of it that surprising, either, I suppose—for most men, nothing is more flattering than having a young person actually pay attention to his advice, and we were no different in that regard. As a result, not a one of us noticed that Wild Bill Wharton was no longer looking up at the ceiling. That includes me, but I know he wasn't. He was looking at us as we stood there by the duty desk, gassing and giving Percy advice. Giving him advice! And him pretending to listen! Quite a laugh, considering how things turned out!

The sound of a key rattling into the lock of the door to the exercise yard put an end to our little post-rehearsal critique. Dean gave Percy a warning glance. "Not a word or a wrong look," he said. "We don't want him to know what we've been doing. It's not good for them. Upsets them."

Percy nodded and ran a finger across his lips in a mum's-the-word gesture that was supposed to be funny and wasn't. The exercise-yard door opened and Delacroix came in, escorted by Brutal, who was carrying the cigar box with the colored spool in it, the way the magician's assistant in a vaudeville show might carry the boss's props offstage at the end of the act. Mr. Jingles was perched on Delacroix's shoulder. And Delacroix himself? I tell you what—Lillie Langtry couldn't have looked any glowier after performing at the White House. "They love Mr. Jingles!"

Delacroix proclaimed. "They laugh and cheer and clap they hands!"

"Well, that's aces," Percy said. He spoke in an indulgent, proprietary way that didn't sound like the old Percy at all. "Pop on back in your cell, old-timer."

Delacroix gave him a comical look of distrust, and the old Percy came busting out. He bared his teeth in a mock snarl and made as if to grab Delacroix. It was a joke, of course, Percy was happy, not in a serious grabbing mood at all, but Delacroix didn't know that. He jerked away with an expression of fear and dismay, and tripped over one of Brutal's big feet. He went down hard, hitting the linoleum with the back of his head. Mr. Jingles leaped away in time to avoid being crushed, and went squeaking off down the Green Mile to Delacroix's cell.

Delacroix got to his feet, gave the chuckling Percy a single hate-filled glance, then scurried off after his pet, calling for him and rubbing the back of his head. Brutal (who didn't know that Percy had shown exciting signs of competency for a change) gave Percy a wordless look of contempt and went after Del, shaking his keys out.

I think what happened next happened because Percy was actually moved to apologize—I know it's hard to believe, but he was in an extraordinary humor that day. If true, it only proves a cynical old adage I heard once, something about how no good deed goes unpunished. Remember me telling you about how, after he'd chased the mouse down to the restraint room on one of those two occasions before

Delacroix joined us, Percy got a little too close to The Pres's cell? Doing that was dangerous, which was why the Green Mile was so wide—when you walked straight down the middle of it, you couldn't be reached from the cells. The Pres hadn't done anything to Percy, but I remember thinking that Arlen Bitterbuck might have, had it been him Percy had gotten too close to. Just to teach him a lesson.

Well, The Pres and The Chief had both moved on, but Wild Bill Wharton had taken their place. He was worse-mannered than The Pres or The Chief had ever dreamed of being, and he'd been watching the whole little play, hoping for a chance to get on stage himself. That chance now fell into his lap, courtesy of Percy Wetmore.

"Hey, Del!" Percy called, half-laughing, starting after Brutal and Delacroix and drifting much too close to Wharton's side of the Green Mile without realizing it. "Hey, you numb shit, I didn't mean nothin by it! Are you all ri—"

Wharton was up off his bunk and over to the bars of his cell in a flash—never in my time as a guard did I see anyone move so fast, and that includes some of the athletic young men Brutal and I worked with later at Boys' Correctional. He shot his arms out through the bars and grabbed Percy, first by the shoulders of his uniform blouse and then by the throat. Wharton dragged him back against his cell door. Percy squealed like a pig in a slaughter-chute, and I saw from his eyes that he thought he was going to die.

"Ain't you sweet," Wharton whispered. One hand left Percy's throat and ruffled through his hair. "Soft!" he said, half-laughing. "Like a girl's. I druther fuck your asshole than your sister's pussy, I think." And he actually kissed Percy's ear.

I think Percy—who had beat Delacroix onto the block for accidentally brushing his crotch, remember—knew exactly what was happening. I doubt that he wanted to, but I think he did. All the color had drained from his face, and the blemishes on his cheeks stood out like birthmarks. His eyes were huge and wet. A line of spittle leaked from one corner of his twitching mouth. All this happened quick—it was begun and done in less than ten seconds, I'd say.

Harry and I stepped forward, our billies raised. Dean drew his gun. But before things could go so much as an inch further, Wharton let go of Percy and stepped back, raising his hands to his shoulders and grinning his dank grin. "I let im go, I 'us just playin and I let im go," he said. "Never hurt airy single hair on that boy's purty head, so don't you go stickin me down in that goddam soft room again."

Percy Wetmore darted across the Green Mile and cringed against the barred door of the empty cell on the other side, breathing so fast and so loud that it sounded almost like sobbing. He had finally gotten his lesson in keeping to the center of the Green Mile and away from the frumious bandersnatch, the teeth that bite and the claws that catch. I had an idea it was a lesson that would stick with him longer than all the advice we'd given him after our rehearsals.

There was an expression of utter terror on his face, and his precious hair was seriously mussed up for the first time since I'd met him, all in spikes and tangles. He looked like someone who has just escaped being raped.

There was a moment of utter stop then, a quiet so thick that the only sound was the sobbing whistle of Percy's breathing. What broke it was cackling laughter, so sudden and so completely its own mad thing that it was shocking. *Wharton* was my first thought, but it wasn't him. It was Delacroix, standing in the open door of his cell and pointing at Percy. The mouse was back on his shoulder, and Delacroix looked like a small but malevolent male witch, complete with imp.

"Lookit him, he done piss his pants!" Delacroix howled. "Lookit what the big man done! Bus' other people wid 'is stick, *mais oui* some *mauvais homme*, but when someone touch him, he make water in 'is pants jus' like a baby!"

He laughed and pointed, all his fear and hatred of Percy coming out in that derisive laughter. Percy stared at him, seemingly incapable of moving or speaking. Wharton stepped back to the bars of his cell, looked down at the dark splotch on the front of Percy's trousers—it was small but it was there, and no question about what it was—and grinned. "Somebody ought to buy the tough boy a didy," he said, and went back to his bunk, chuffing laughter.

Brutal went down to Delacroix's cell, but the Cajun

had ducked inside and thrown himself on his bunk before Brutal could get there.

I reached out and grasped Percy's shoulder. "Percy—" I began, but that was as far as I got. He came to life, shaking my hand off. He looked down at the front of his pants, saw the spot spreading there, and blushed a dark, fiery red. He looked up at me again, then at Harry and Dean. I remember being glad that Old Toot-Toot was gone. If he'd been around, the story would have been all over the prison in a single day. And, given Percy's last name—an unfortunate one, in this context—it was a story that would have been told with the relish of high glee for years to come.

"You talk about this to anyone, and you'll all be on the breadlines in a week," he whispered fiercely. It was the sort of crack that would have made me want to swat him under other circumstances, but under these, I only pitied him. I think he saw that pity, and it made it worse with him—like having an open wound scoured with nettles.

"What goes on here stays here," Dean said quietly. "You don't have to worry about that."

Percy looked back over his shoulder, toward Delacroix's cell. Brutal was just locking the door, and from inside, deadly clear, we could still hear Delacroix giggling. Percy's look was as black as thunder. I thought of telling him that you reaped what you sowed in this life, and then decided this might not be the right time for a scripture lesson.

"As for him—" he began, but never finished. He

left, instead, head down, to go into the storage room and look for a dry pair of pants.

"He's so *purty*," Wharton said in a dreamy voice. Harry told him to shut the fuck up before he went down to the restraint room just on general damned principles. Wharton folded his arms on his chest, closed his eyes, and appeared to go to sleep.

9

The night before Delacroix's execution came down hotter and muggier than ever—eighty-one degrees by the thermometer outside the Admin ready-room window when I clocked in at six. Eighty-one degrees at the end of October, think of that, and thunder rumbling in the west like it does in July. I'd met a member of my congregation in town that afternoon, and he had asked me, with apparent seriousness, if I thought such unseasonable weather could be a sign of the Last Times. I said that I was sure not, but it crossed my mind that it was Last Times for Eduard Delacroix, all right. Yes indeed it was.

Bill Dodge was standing in the door to the exercise yard, drinking coffee and smoking him a little smoke. He looked around at me and said, "Well, lookit here. Paul Edgecombe, big as life and twice as ugly."

"How'd the day go, Billy?"

"All right."

"Delacroix?"

"Fine. He seems to understand it's tomorrow, and

yet it's like he *don't* understand. You know how most of em are when the end finally comes for them."

I nodded. "Wharton?"

Bill laughed. "What a comedian. Makes Jack Benny sound like a Quaker. He told Rolfe Wettermark that he ate strawberry jam out of his wife's pussy."

"What did Rolfe say?"

"That he wasn't married. Said it must have been his mother Wharton was thinking of."

I laughed, and hard. That really was funny, in a low sort of way. And it was good just to be able to laugh without feeling like someone was lighting matches way down low in my gut. Bill laughed with me, then turned the rest of his coffee out in the yard, which was empty except for a few shuffling trusties, most of whom had been there for a thousand years or so.

Thunder rumbled somewhere far off, and unfocused heat lightning flashed in the darkening sky overhead. Bill looked up uneasily, his laughter dying.

"I tell you what, though," he said, "I don't like this weather much. Feels like something's gonna happen. Something bad."

About that he was right. The bad thing happened right around quarter of ten that night. That was when Percy killed Mr. Jingles.

10

At first it seemed like it was going to be a pretty good night in spite of the heat—John Coffey was being his usual quiet self, Wild Bill was making out to be Mild Bill, and Delacroix was in good spirits for a man who had a date with Old Sparky in a little more than twenty-four hours.

He *did* understand what was going to happen to him, at least on the most basic level; he had ordered chili for his last meal and gave me special instructions for the kitchen. "Tell em to lay on dat hot-sauce," he said. "Tell em the kind dat really jump up your t'roat an' say howdy—the green stuff, none of dat mild. Dat stuff gripe me like a motherfucker, I can't get off the toilet the nex' day, but I don't think I gonna have a problem this time, *n'est-ce pas?*"

Most of them worry about their immortal souls with a kind of moronic ferocity, but Delacroix pretty much dismissed my questions about what he wanted for spiritual comfort in his last hours. If "dat fella" Schuster had been good enough for Big Chief Bitterbuck, Del reckoned, Schuster would be good enough for him. No, what he cared about—you've guessed already, I'm sure—was what was going to happen to Mr. Jingles after he, Delacroix, passed on. I was used to spending long hours with the condemned on the night before their last march, but this was the first time I'd spent those long hours pondering the fate of a mouse.

Del considered scenario after scenario, patiently working the possibilities through his dim mind. And while he thought aloud, wanting to provide for his pet mouse's future as if it were a child that had to be put through college, he threw that colored spool against the wall. Each time he did it, Mr. Jingles would spring after it, track it down, and then roll it back to Del's foot. It started to get on my nerves after awhile—first the clack of the spool against the stone wall, then the minute clitter of Mr. Jingles's paws. Although it was a cute trick, it palled after ninety minutes or so. And Mr. Jingles never seemed to get tired. He paused every now and then to refresh himself with a drink of water out of a coffee saucer Delacroix kept for just that purpose, or to munch a pink crumb of peppermint candy, and then back to it he went. Several times it was on the tip of my tongue to tell Delacroix to give it a rest, and each time I reminded myself that he had this night and tomorrow to play the spool-game with Mr. Jingles, and that was all. Near the end, though, it began to be really difficult to hold onto that thought—you know how it is, with a noise that's repeated over and over. After a while it shoots your nerve. I started to speak after all, then something made me look over my shoulder and out the cell door. John Coffey was standing at *his* cell door across the way, and he shook his head at me: right, left, back to center. As if he had read my mind and was telling me to think again.

I would see that Mr. Jingles got to Delacroix's maiden aunt, I said, the one who had sent him the big bag of candy. His colored spool could go as well, even his "house"—we'd take up a collection and see that Toot gave up his claim on the Corona box. No, said Delacroix after some consideration (he had time to throw the spool against the wall at least five times, with Mr. Jingles either nosing it back or pushing it with his paws), that wouldn't do. Aunt Hermione was too old, she wouldn't understand Mr. Jingles's frisky ways, and suppose Mr. Jingles outlived her? What would happen to him then? No, no, Aunt Hermione just wouldn't do.

Well, then, I asked, suppose one of us took it? One of us guards? We could keep him right here on E Block. No, Delacroix said, he thanked me kindly for the thought, *certainement*, but Mr. Jingles was a mouse that yearned to be free. He, Eduard Delacroix, knew this, because Mr. Jingles had—you guessed it— whispered the information in his ear.

"All right," I said, "one of us will take him home, Del. Dean, maybe. He's got a little boy that would just love a pet mouse, I bet."

Delacroix actually turned pale with horror at the thought. A little kid in charge of a rodent genius like Mr. Jingles? How in the name of *le bon Dieu* could a little kid be expected to keep up with his training, let alone teach him new tricks? And suppose the kid lost interest and forgot to feed him for two or three days at a stretch? Delacroix, who had roasted six human beings alive in an effort to cover up his original crime, shuddered with the delicate revulsion of an ardent anti-vivisectionist.

All right, I said, I'd take him myself (promise them anything, remember; in their last forty-eight hours, promise them anything). How would that be?

"No, sir, Boss Edgecombe," Del said apologetically. He threw the spool again. It hit the wall, bounced, spun; then Mr. Jingles was on it like white on rice and nosing it back to Delacroix. "Thank you kindly— *merci beaucoup*—but you live out in the woods, and Mr. Jingles, he be scared to live out *dans la forêt*. I know, because—"

"I think I can guess how you know, Del," I said.

Delacroix nodded, smiling. "But we gonna figure this out. You bet!" He threw the spool. Mr. Jingles clittered after it. I tried not to wince.

In the end it was Brutal who saved the day. He had been up by the duty desk, watching Dean and Harry play cribbage. Percy was there, too, and Brutal finally tired of trying to start a conversation with him and getting nothing but sullen grunts in response. He strolled down to where I sat on a stool outside of Delacroix's cell and stood there listening to us with his arms folded.

"How about Mouseville?" Brutal asked into the considering silence which followed Del's rejection of my spooky old house out in the woods. He threw the comment out in a casual just-an-idea tone of voice.

"Mouseville?" Delacroix asked, giving Brutal a look both startled and interested. "What Mouseville?"

"It's this tourist attraction down in Florida," he said. "Tallahassee, I think. Is that right, Paul? Tallahassee?"

"Yep," I said, speaking without a moment's hesitation, thinking God bless Brutus Howell. "Tallahassee. Right down the road apiece from the dog university." Brutal's mouth twitched at that, and I thought he was going to queer the pitch by laughing, but he got it under control and nodded. I'd hear about the dog university later, though, I imagined.

This time Del didn't throw the spool, although Mr. Jingles stood on Del's slipper with his front paws raised, clearly lusting for another chance to chase. The Cajun looked from Brutal to me and back to Brutal again. "What dey do in Mouseville?" he asked.

"You think they'd take Mr. Jingles?" Brutal asked me, simultaneously ignoring Del and drawing him on. "Think he's got the stuff, Paul?"

I tried to appear considering. "You know," I said, "the more I think of it, the more it seems like a brilliant idea." From the corner of my eye I saw Percy come partway down the Green Mile (giving Wharton's cell a very wide berth). He stood with one shoulder leaning against an empty cell, listening with a small, contemptuous smile on his lips.

"What dis Mouseville?" Del asked, now frantic to know.

"A tourist attraction, like I told you," Brutal said. "There's, oh I dunno, a hundred or so mice there. Wouldn't you say, Paul?"

"More like a hundred and fifty these days," I said. "It's a big success. I understand they're thinking of opening one out in California and calling it Mouseville West, that's how much business is booming. Trained mice are the coming thing with the smart set, I guess—I don't understand it, myself."

Del sat with the colored spool in his hand, looking at us, his own situation forgotten for the time being.

"They only take the smartest mice," Brutal cautioned, "the ones that can do tricks. And they can't be white mice, because those are pet-shop mice."

"Pet-shop mice, yeah, you bet!" Delacroix said fiercely. "I hate dem pet-shop mice!"

"And what they got," Brutal said, his eyes distant now as he imagined it, "is this tent you go into—"

"Yeah, yeah, like inna *cirque*! Do you gotta pay to get in?"

"You shittin me? *Course* you gotta pay to get in. A dime apiece, two cents for the kiddies. And there's, like, this whole city made out of Bakelite boxes and toilet-paper rolls, with windows made out of isinglass so you can see what they're up to in there—"

"Yeah! Yeah!" Delacroix was in ecstasy now. Then he turned to me. "What ivy-glass?"

"Like on the front of a stove, where you can see in," I said.

"Oh sure! Dat shit!" He cranked his hand at Brutal, wanting him to go on, and Mr. Jingles's little oildrop eyes practically spun in their sockets, trying to keep that spool in view. It was pretty funny. Percy came a little closer, as if wanting to get a better look, and I saw John Coffey frowning at him, but I was too wrapped up in Brutal's fantasy to pay much attention. This took telling the condemned man what he wanted to hear to new heights, and I was all admiration, believe me.

"Well," Brutal said, "there's the mouse city, but what the kids really like is the Mouseville All-Star Circus, where there's mice that swing on trapezes, and mice that roll these little barrels, and mice that stack coins—"

"Yeah, dat's it! Dat's the place for Mr. Jingles!" Delacroix said. His eyes sparkled and his cheeks were high with color. It occurred to me that Brutus Howell was a kind of saint. "You gonna be a circus mouse after all, Mr. Jingles! Gonna live in a mouse city down Florida! All ivy-glass windows! Hurrah!"

He threw the spool extra-hard. It hit low on the wall, took a crazy bounce, and squirted out between the bars of his cell door and onto the Mile. Mr. Jingles raced out after it, and Percy saw his chance.

"*No, you fool!*" Brutal yelled, but Percy paid no attention. Just as Mr. Jingles reached the spool—too intent on it to realize his old enemy was at hand—Percy brought the sole of one hard black workshoe down on it. There was an audible snap as Mr. Jingles's back broke, and blood gushed from his mouth. His tiny dark eyes bulged in their sockets, and in them I read an expression of surprised agony that was all too human.

Delacroix screamed with horror and grief. He threw himself at the door of his cell and thrust his arms out between the bars, reaching as far as he could, crying the mouse's name over and over.

Percy turned toward him, smiling. Toward the three of us. "There," he said. "I knew I'd get him, sooner or later. Just a matter of time, really." He turned and walked back up the Green Mile, not hurrying, leaving Mr. Jingles lying on the linoleum in a spreading pool of his own blood.

To Be Continued

THE GREAT ESCAPE

Stay tuned to *The Green Mile* serial thriller for your
chance to WIN over 1,000 AIR MILES awards in each
episode up to Part 5, with a massive 6,000 AIR MILES
awards to be won in Part 6 for the greatest escape ever!

COMPETITION No.3

WIN 1,003 AIR MILES AWARDS PLUS

A SPECIAL EDITION OF THE NEXT EPISODE,

The Bad Death of Eduard Delacroix,

SIGNED BY STEPHEN KING

Call 0881 88 77 66

with your answers to the following questions and you could
escape to a destination of your choice.

Which of the following events will happen in the next episode...

1. John Coffey saves Mr Jingles with his magic power.

2. Percy Wetmore apologizes to Delacroix for being mean.

3. Mr Jingles retires to Florida.

Tie-Breaker:

In 20 words or less, describe the continuing plot of *The Green Mile*...

Telephone lines close MIDNIGHT 20 June 1996

*The serial thriller continues
next month . . .*

STEPHEN KING'S
THE GREEN MILE:
Part Four
The Bad Death of
Eduard Delacroix

Time has run out for one of the inmates at Cold
Mountain. Eduard Delacroix is set to take that final
walk down the Green Mile. But first he must say
goodbye, to the guards, to the other inmates, and to
the small creature that forever changed his life. Little
does he know of the terrible fate that awaits him,
and of a devilish plan of revenge . . .

To Be Continued . . .